First Printing, 2022

To my wife Erica and our children Blake and Ivy.
Keep pushing through when the going gets tough!

The night before the big race and little Blake was a mess,
The tears rolled down his face from all of the stress.

Thoughts kept running wild all through his mind.
What if I'm slow, so far behind?
What if I'm late? What if I lose?
What if I fall or lose my shoes?

Blake's dad sat him down while he was still cryin'
He said, "Be a brave little man, just like a lion!"
"Be fierce, and be tough, just go out and run
and don't worry at all because it's about having fun."

But Blake didn't feel fierce, and he didn't feel tough.
He was scared of the race and that was enough.
He looked up at his dad right in the eye
And softly asked, "Do lions cry?"

What an open-ended question to ask right before bed.
Blake's dad knew the answers, to help clear his son's head.
So, without hesitation this is what he said:

Does the king of the jungle get scared and sometimes upset?
Does the king of the jungle worry and fret?
YOU BET!

When the female lions hunt for dinner at night
You can guarantee that in their mind is some fright.
But they don't let it stop them, they just push on through.
And when you get scared, that is what you should do.

When lions get lonely, I am sure they get sad.
Away from their home, their mom, and their dad.
But they don't let it stop them, they just push on through.
And when you get sad, that is what you should do.

A lion's roar is so loud it can be heard for miles.
While there aren't any actual tears, this cry goes on for a while.
They are just like a baby, seeking attention from others.
Making loud noises with their sisters and brothers.

You see, lions might be the king of them all
But even at times, a lion feels small.
But they don't let it stop them, they just push on through
And when you get these feelings, that is what you should do!

So even when a lion might be filled with fright,
They don't let others know, they keep it sealed tight.
They try to stand tall and puff out their chest.
Fill themselves with confidence to do their best.

There are things you can control that
will help your stress be relieved.
Count to ten slowly and listen to yourself
breathe.
Before the race starts, sing a song in
your head,
Or think of a funny joke that someone
once said.
Imagine yourself relaxing, so calm and
so free
And watch as you go from doubt to
belief.

Blake drifted off to sleep with a smile on his face.
He was ready to overcome these emotions and dominate his race!

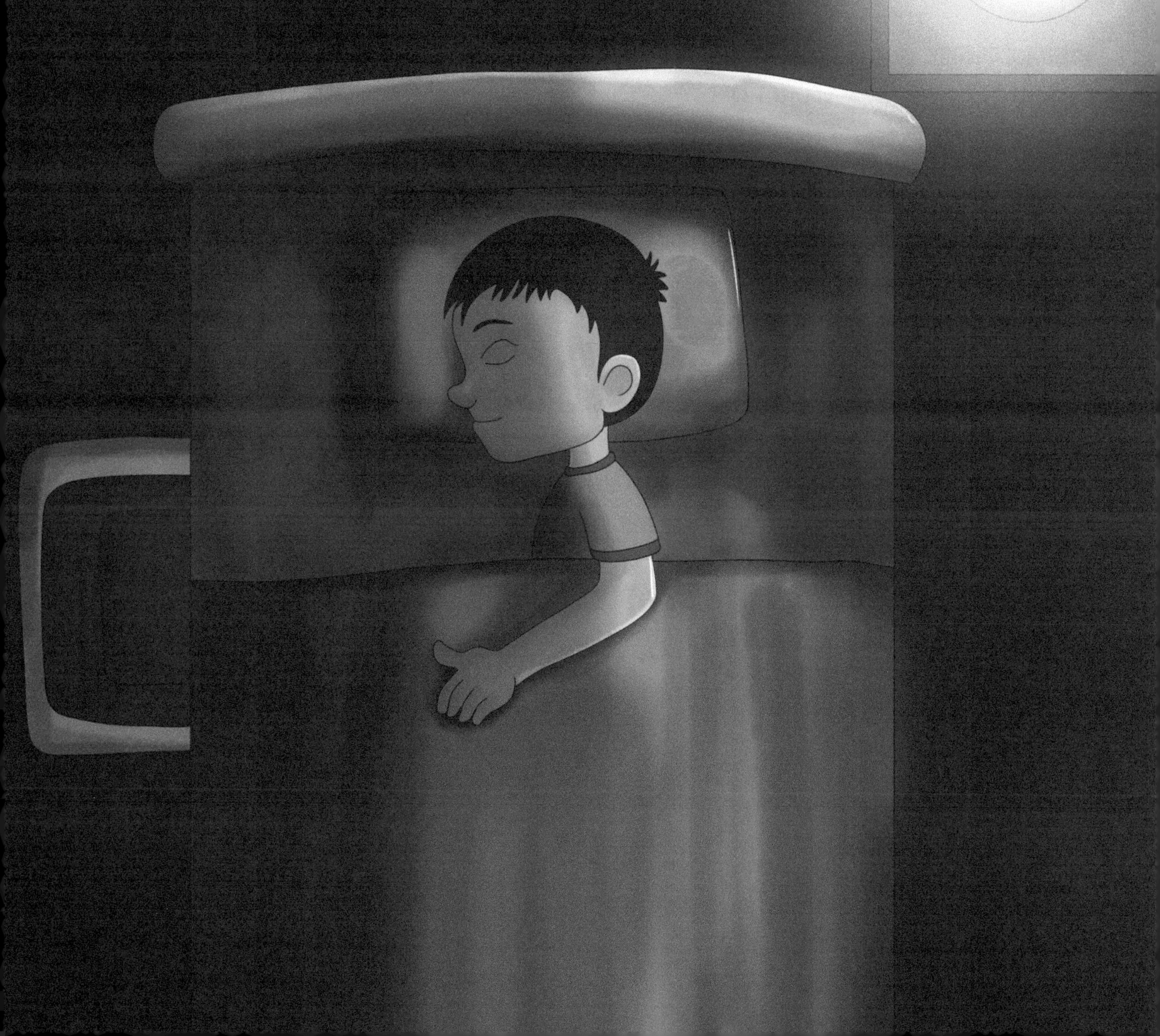

Blake woke up ready to take on this race,
Stood looking in the mirror at his game face.
He tried to stand tall and puff out his chest.
Filled himself with confidence, ready to do his best.
"You got this!" he told himself with a grin,
He was ready for this race to begin.

Race time was here, and Blake held his head high.
But as he approached the starting line he wanted to cry.
He itched and he scratched, and he wiggled around
But at that moment, his courage was found.

He counted to ten and sang in his head,
And remembered the talk with his dad in his bed.
He thought about the lions his dad told him about
And at that moment he heard someone shout.
"GO!" said the woman, the race had begun.
There was no more time for thinking, it was time to RUN!

The ROAR from the crowd could be heard for miles.
As Blake sprinted toward the finish line, he was all smiles.
He was scared, intimidated, and tired, but he knew what to do.
He pictured himself as a lion, just pushing on through.

Blake was embraced by his parents, and here's what they said:
"We knew you could do it once you cleared your head.
It's normal to have these feelings, that try to hold you back
Whether it's trying new things, going to strange places, or running around a track."

Blake smiled and laughed now that it was all done.
He had a great time, so glad that he had run.
But as he stood there with his medal, proud as can be
His little sister cried with nothing but great envy.

"It's not fair! I want a medal!" she yelled with a hiss.
Now this was another opportunity that her dad would not miss.
"Ivy my dear don't cry, you know what to do?
Remember those penguins you love from the zoo?
They are always splashing, playing, and having a blast
Act like a penguin and cheer up real
fast!"

Ivy looked at her dad unsure what
the penguin thing was about.
Then looked at her dad and
asked, "Do penguins pout?"

### Before Reading

Having students share about a time they were nervous or scared to do something, will help children connect to the main character of the story. Have students write or verbally share.

How do you deal with these emotions? What did you do to overcome your fears?

### During Reading

There are many ways this story can be used in a classroom. Some literary elements that can be discussed throughout the book are:
- Cause and Effect
- Problem & Solution
- Story Structure
- Figurative Language (Metaphors, Similes)
- Rhyme Scheme
- Making Connections
- Conflict (Person vs Person, Person vs Self, Person vs Nature, Person vs Society)

### After Reading Activities

How did Blake overcome his conflict?

What strategies can you use when feeling stressed, anxious, or scared?

Write/Draw a time when you felt like Blake? How did you solve your problem?

Review the "calming" strategies from pg 16. Have students practice these strategies in class.

Have students research lions and gather facts about lions. Have them answer the question: Do they cry?

Phil Lockwood has been an educator in a K-8 setting for the last 14 years. With a degree in Elementary Education and two Masters Degrees in Literacy (K-12) and Educational Leadership, Phil relied on his knowledge and experience in the education field to help write this story. Knowing first hand that children deal with a lot of anxiety and stress, Phil wrote Do Lions Cry? to offer help to those who could use it. The story is based on real life events with his son Blake. When Blake first started races he was very fast but would often "freeze" with anxiety at the starting line. We are happy to report that Blake has learned techniques and strategies to help him conquer his fears on the track! Phil lives in Palisades, NY with his wife Erica and their children Blake & Ivy. He also owns a private tutoring business called **Teachers to the Rescue** which works with students throughout New York and New Jersey.

Blake getting ready to overcome his fears and run the race!

Blake showing off his trophy!

CPSIA information can be obtained
at www.ICGtesting.com
Printed in the USA
BVHW021059090422
633507BV00004B/100